Shadows Never Lie

AMY LAURENS

OTHER WORKS

Find other works by the author at www.amylaurens.com

Shadows Never Lie

INKLET #79

AMY LAURENS

Inkprint
PRESS

www.inkprintpress.com

Print ISBN: 978-1-922434-19-7
eBook ISBN: 9798201924782

www.inkprintpress.com

National Library of Australia Cataloguing-in-Publication Data
Laurens, Amy 1985 –
Shadows Never Lie
52 p.
ISBN: 978-1-922434-19-7
Inkprint Press, Canberra, Australia
1. Fiction—Fantasy—Contemporary 2. Fiction—Short Stories

First Print Edition: April 2022
Cover photo © Pavel Kolotenko via Deposit Photos
Cover design © Inkprint Press
Interior art © Amy Laurens

SHADOWS NEVER LIE

CRACKPOTS AND STALKERS

It's the shadows that tell you who someone really is, much more than what they look like or even how they act. People can train themselves to cover up anything; but the shadows never lie. Of course, I couldn't always see the shadows. It took my own shift to realise how. But once I knew, I could never go back to how I had been—even if it meant I had to live with my own shadow.

CANDANCE RAN DOWN THE STREET, brown hair slicked back in a ponytail, sweat sheening her forehead and dripping down her cleavage.

The late evening sun melted over the street, turning everything honey-coloured, and everyone else seemed to react by becoming slow themselves, like the light had turned viscous. Candance alone sped through the evening, keen to get her jog over and done with so she could hit the shower and get ready for dinner.

Usually, jogging was enough to let her zone out and forget the worries of the day; this evening, not so much. Flashes of deep blue satin, glimmerings of diamonds and the faint rush of applause intruded on her quiet, threatening to steal her concentration away entirely.

Frustrated, Candance ground her teeth and pounded harder against the pavement. *I will not be distracted,* she told herself. *I will not be distracted.*

The conflicting scents of hot tar, exhaust fumes, and freshly cut grass mingled in the air, and she breathed deeply, counting out her strides as she did. In-one-two-three, out-one-two-three, and on and on down the street until formal dinners faded from mind and she forgot about everything except her feet hitting the concrete, her arms pumping at her sides and the steady rhythm of her breaths.

She turned the final corner for home feeling more centred than she'd managed all week—and cried out as she ran into a person standing hunched in the middle of the path. A crack in the pavement seemed to leap up and tangle itself around her toes, and before she knew it, Candance's palms scraped the ground, quickly followed by her knees.

Hissing, she lifted her hands to survey the damage. Fine gravel had embedded in her skin and the heels of her palms bled. Her knees weren't much better. Wincing, she struggled to her feet. *Well, this is going to look amazing with my gown,* she thought, and pursed her lips.

"You shouldn't go, you know," said a voice, and Candance whirled to face the stranger. A woman, though her voice had been deep enough to belong to a man, old but not frail, hunched but not weakened.

"Go where?"

"To the dinner tonight."

Candance's heart leapt in her chest. "How do you know about the dinner?"

The woman simply shrugged. "Don't go."

Heart pounding now with adrenalin as well as exertion, Candance licked her lips. "That's none of your business." She turned away.

"Suit yourself," said the woman. "Most people prefer not to have an audience is all. Don't say I didn't warn you."

Candance stopped, struggling. On the one hand, the woman was obviously a crackpot at best, and a stalker at worst.

On the other... "Why not?" she said at last, back still to the woman.

"You haven't felt it waking?" the woman asked in apparent surprise.

"Felt what?" Irritation blossomed. Stupid woman, standing around where people could run into her, making vague prognostications and being obtuse. *Why am I even still listening?*

"You truly do not know what you are?" The woman shuffled into Candance's peripheral vision and peered at her. "How strange."

What I am? Candance shuddered, squashing the fear that was trying to take root in the back of her mind. "I have no idea what you're talking about. I'm leaving now." She launched back into a jog, wondering why she'd even felt the need to respond. She should have just ignored the woman from the start, kept jogging and not listened to a thing. She glanced back over her shoulder, pulse skipping when she accidentally made eye contact with the woman.

"Don't go," the woman called again. "It's waking. I can see your shadow, even if you can't."

Candance's gaze flicked down to her shadow in front of her. She frowned. It was a perfectly average shadow, and she could see it perfectly well. What on earth...? And even more strange, when she glanced back again, curious despite herself, the woman had gone.

Oh well, Candance thought, rolling her neck as she ran. *Don't think about it. Pretend it didn't happen.* She shoved aside the uneasiness and told herself it was only nerves.

QUICKENING

The thing about pretending is that we all do it. We all pretend to be something we're not, and we do it most of the time without even thinking. And yet the very first thing we look for in a mate is someone we don't have to pretend with, someone we can be our deepest, realest selves around.

I sometimes wonder what the world would be like if we all just stopped pretending. Then I remember the shadows, and know: sometimes, the only thing standing between civilisation and anarchy is our willingness to pretend.

CANDANCE SMOOTHED THE FINAL HAIR-pin into place and surveyed the result in the mirror. A triple strand of diamantes encircled her neck and another circled one wrist; genuine diamond-encrusted hairpins accented her updo. The midnight satin gown glimmered softly under the lights of her bathroom and she allowed her lips to quirk up slightly at the corners. She scrubbed up okay.

She headed back through the bedroom, snagging shoes on the way, and paused in the front entryway to slip them on just as someone knocked at the door. "Coming," she called as she did up the final buckle and tottered to the door.

"Allen, hi," she said as he grinned and proffered a cream rose in full bloom. She tapped the front of her left shoulder and leaned forward as Allen pinned it onto her dress.

"Stunning," he pronounced, and offered her his arm.

Grinning in return, Candance took it and allowed him to lead her toward the car. Allen had taken her under his wing five years ago when she'd first arrived in town. They'd hit it off right away, in a friendly, brother-sister sort of way, and Candance hadn't been at all surprised when he'd first introduced her to his boyfriend. Five years later, Allen and she were better friends than ever, and he'd been the easy choice for an escort to this evening's do, where any other invitation might be seen as a serious proposal on her behalf, and turning up alone was impermissible.

Candance paused as Allen stooped to open the car, all prepared to flash him a charming smile and slide into the front seat; instead, she frowned as something unfamiliar surged through her stomach. It almost felt like the lurch of adrenalin, only it was hotter, quicker, there-and-then-gone.

"Are you okay?"

Candance pretended she'd just been smoothing down her skirt.

"Of course."

She gave him the planned smile and climbed into the car, stiffening as the strange sensation seized her again.

Allen closed her door and rounded the front of the car to climb into the driver's seat. "All set?" he asked, looking her up and down. His eyes lingered over her stomach and his lips tightened into the barest suggestion of a frown. "Are you sure you want to go tonight?"

Candance knitted her brows. "Of course I am. I have to go. I *want* to go. I—" She cut off and hissed as the feeling surged again, this time with a hot edge of pain.

Allen raised an eyebrow and glanced pointedly at Candance's hands, which now clutched her belly. "It's all under control?"

"Of course." She'd eaten something funny, or maybe overdone the run, that was all. It was nothing. She'd be fine.

"So, tell me about the fabulous speech you'll be making tonight," Allen said, turning the key in the ignition and pulling smoothly out into the street.

Candance leaned back and closed her eyes. A feeling of well-practiced calm soothed over her and she smiled, anticipating the moment. "I can't believe they chose me."

Allen laughed. "Probably not the best way to begin."

She laughed with him. "No, probably not."

Still, it was the truth: she'd been surprised enough when her boss had told her that she'd been nominated for the prestigious ATS Santo Award for her research into the social behaviour of oceanic bearded dragons. The news that she'd won had been almost beyond belief.

Candance gasped as her stomach contracted. She tightened her fingers convulsively and Allen shot her a worried glance.

She smiled back at him. "I'll start

with the story about the dragon biting my finger when I was in Hawaii that time." *Please ignore it,* she begged him with her eyes. Tonight, of all nights, everything had to be perfect. She'd worked so hard...

Her aunt's voice rang in her ears, reminding her that of all the people who'd tried to make a name for themselves in marine herpetology, only three were currently making a job of it.

Allen nodded and focused on the road ahead, worry still tightening the corners of his mouth and eyes—but at least he'd let it go for now.

Candance knotted her fingers in her lap. "Then," she continued, ignoring the tremors in her belly that felt like her last meal was trying to escape, "after they're all dying of laughter at me, I'll turn on the serious-face charm," she tested it out on Allen, eyes wide and serious, "and they'll love me. Right?"

He reached out and lightly punched her shoulder. "They'll adore you."

Twenty minutes later they pulled up outside the Princeton Hotel, a giant, fifty-storey affair spangled in gold and purple lighting and backdropped by the Bellington Wharf, home to all boats worth more than Candance's house. Candance popped the passenger door open and stretched one leg out. Cramps hit her in the stomach like knives, and she doubled over.

Allen grabbed her wrist and turned her, searching her face. "You don't have to do this," he said. "Not tonight."

Candance glanced up to where her boss stood waiting at the top of the stairs, and heard her aunt once again. "Yes," she said, straightening, teeth gritted as she forced away the pain. "I do."

"Candance, you can walk away from this. We can leave—"

She shook her head. "I can't do that to them."

"Sure you can, we just—"

"Look, I'm going, alright?" she snapped as another wave of nausea flooded over her. Nausea was better than pain. She exhaled. "Sorry. I'm going. They're expecting me, this is a big deal, and I can't just walk away. I won't," she added.

Candance stared across at Allen and put a hand on his shoulder. "I appreciate your concern," she said, softly now. "But if I leave, it's not just the ceremony I'm walking away from. It's the Award, my job... everything." Tears welled in her eyes. "I can't just walk away."

"Okay," he replied just as softly. He squeezed her arm. "You can do this."

Candance nodded and swiped away the tear.

"Go get 'em, tiger." Allen grinned. "I'll meet you in there shortly."

Candance watched him drive away towards the car park, then turned to face the hotel, stomach flipping from nausea—and nerves.

THE BEAST WITHIN

I used to wish I'd listened to Allen, that night. But then I wonder what would have happened if I had. I might still have my job, for one thing. And the Award. That was what hit me hardest afterwards—Aunt Clarisse had been right. My chosen career path was a complete dead end.

She was wrong about the rest, though.

I wouldn't go back for the world.

"AND NOW," SAID THE PRESENTER ON stage while the lights glimmered off his perfectly coiffed hair, "the winner of the ATS Santo Award, Candance Murray!"

The crowd erupted into applause like a flight of gem-toned butterflies. Candance pushed her chair back and stood, demurring as Allen offered his arm and her table companions offered their congratulations. Her stomach fluttered and Candance smoothed her hands over her belly as she glided up to the front.

The first two steps proved no obstacle, but on the third, while the crowd still cheered behind her, the same stabbing pain from the car earlier ripped through Candance's gut, and she stumbled. A few members of the crowd gasped as Candance struggled to right herself, the floor swimming before her eyes.

No, she told herself. *Come on. Get up there and thank them. You can't fall apart now.*

Candance forced herself upright, clinging to the narrow handrail. Gritting her teeth, she conquered the final two steps and strode to the podium, her shadow dancing under her feet, flung every way by the multi-directional lighting.

The walk to the podium took years, and by the time she reached it, the applause had well and truly died. Candance's cheeks felt burningly hot, and as she clutched at the podium for support she wished the presenter would just hold the stupid trophy still so she could claim it. And why did he have to wave it about in that ridiculous manner anyway?

He leaned towards her. "Are you okay?"

"Of course I'm okay," Candance snapped, reaching for the award. "Give me that."

He frowned, but passed the slab of glass on its wooden mount to her and guided her to the microphone. "Candance Murray!" he said again, and the room broke into over-enthusiastic applause underscored by a riot of whispers.

Candance swallowed, wetting her throat, and opened her mouth. Instead of the thank you she'd intended, she groaned as another bout of pain stabbed through her. Over the podium, her shadow flickered. Candance stared. She really must be unwell; for a moment it had looked like she'd grown a snout. She shook her head and tried again. "Thank you," she said. Her voice sounded gravelly and raw. "It's an honour to... receive..." She tried to remember what the award was called.

Allen rose from their table and started towards her, weaving between chairs, eyes fixed on her. Candance smiled. Sweet of him to come help her with her speech. She didn't need help, though; she was doing just fine. Why, the entire audience was holding their collective breath, just waiting to see what she'd say next! She grinned at them, then blinked in surprise at the slab of glass in her hand. She frowned. "What's this?"

The presenter stretched his lips, but Candance could tell that he was unhappy. Something about the eyes and the way that he tried to usher her away from the podium. Probably it was this stupid glass thing they'd given her. The nausea in her stomach was making it hard to think, but really, who in their right mind would have made such an ugly, misshapen lump?

Allen reached the bottom of the podium and hissed out her name. "Candance! Come down here!"

The presenter pushed her towards Allen, so she took one hesitant step, then another.

Allen smiled encouragingly. "That's right, just keep coming."

Halfway to him, Candance gagged and retched as something tried to claw its way through her stomach. The award dropped to the floor with a heavy thud, and Candance followed.

Allen's arms wrapped around her and he shoved something at her mouth. "Swallow this," he whispered urgently. "Now!"

Candance gulped the sticky paste down, then gagged again as Allen hauled her to her feet.

"No," Allen said, brushing the presenter aside. "I'll just take her out for some fresh air. I'm sure she'll be fine. You just carry on," he added when the presenter looked lost.

"No," Candance gasped as she stubbed her foot on the award and it rolled away. "No, I need that." She couldn't quite remember why, but the burning need was there.

"We're a bit past that, don't you think?" Allen muttered as he steered her by the elbow towards the nearest exit. "Just get out of here. I don't know what on earth you were thinking, coming tonight. I should never have let you leave the house."

Abruptly Candance realised that her cheeks were cold because they were now outside; the wind was cooling tears on her face. "No," she whispered.

Pain wracked through her body again, and for an instant her shadow flickered, something huge and toothy and clawed.

For just that instant, Candance reeled in shock; she knew what was trying to claw its way out of her stomach. Eyes wide, terror slicking her palms, Candance turned to Allen. "What's happening to me?"

Allen stopped short and stared at her. "What do you mean?"

She trembled. "Allen, I feel like... like something is trying to rip my stomach out." *And like I'm about a hairsbreadth away from turning into a monster.* "What's—" Her words were lost in a growl as her teeth flashed,

long and needle sharp, and her body
billowed to something twelve feet tall
and scaly before plummeting her back
into her own skin.

Candance reeled.

Allen caught her arm and steadied
her before leading her out towards the
farthest wharf. "Here," he said as they
paused where the paving met wooden
slats. "Eat more of this. It'll help keep
it under control."

"But what *is* it?" Candance said over
a tongueful of the sweet, sticky paste.
She swallowed and felt the beast in her
stomach settle a little.

Allen heaved an almighty sigh, then
stalked off down the wharf.

Candance followed. "What is it?"
she asked, unable to sort the fluttering
and palpitating into neat categories of
sick and nerves and beast. "What's
wrong with me?"

Allen sighed again and ran a hand
over his head. "Nothing's wrong with

you. You're changing."

"Changing?"

"Your beast," he said. "It's breaking free. You're changing. Did you see your shadow flickering before? I saw that at your house, when I gave you the rose, and knew it was coming, but I didn't expect it to be this fast." His hand ran over his hair again.

Candance clenched her teeth and glared. "What do you mean, changing? And if you knew something was wrong with me, why didn't you say something earlier, in the car?"

"I thought you knew!"

Candance cocked her head. "What, that I had a monstrous beast lurking inside of me, just waiting to break free?"

"No!" Allen threw his hands up. "That you're a theriomorph. A shape-shifter. It runs in families; I assumed your parents would have prepared you."

Candance reeled, head pounding, stomach still roiling. Somewhere out in the darkness, a curlew called. "My parents died when I was eight."

"Oh."

The silence stretched again, broken only by the cries of the curlew and the lap-lap-lap of water against the wharf.

He's thinking about me, Candance thought. *He's wondering how to tell me I've become a monster and he doesn't want to be friends anymore.* Suddenly, that seemed like the worst thing that could possibly happen, far worse than turning into a monster, or even people knowing she turned into one. 'People' was amorphous, nebulous; Allen was *Allen.*

"So," she said, aiming for casual as she leaned back against the wharf's railing and hooked her arms around it. "Other than the fact that I was clearly making a fool of myself, why whip me out here and feed me that... stuff?" Her heart hammered. "Also," she said, straightening, "how did you know to do that?"

Allen seemed to take his time thinking, turning to link his arms through the railing next to her and surveying the stars. "The paste slows the transition, makes it more controllable and less painful. It's a relatively new invention. As for the other, I could see that you were about to change, and..." He shrugged. "We never show ourselves in public."

"We?" Candance cut in. "You're one too?"

"Yes. A grey fox." He weaved his head and caught her gaze. "Are you listening to me? We *don't show ourselves*. It's safer that way. Especially for the more unusual"—he shot her a glance—"of us." He frowned. "What are you, anyway? A lizard?"

Candance smirked, eyes narrowing. She'd only had an instant to meet her inner animal, but an instant had been all she'd needed. "A lizard?" she asked cuttingly. "Really?"

The change bubbled up inside again, and this time she knew it wouldn't be suppressed; it was too strong, too hot, and holding it in would scorch her from the inside out.

So this time, she let it go, laughing in delight as the power swirled up from her belly, around her chest, and tingled down her arms and legs.

Suffused with the warm light of change, her fingernails shot out and claws punched the air, one quickly after the other, a staccato of rifle shots. Muscles stretched, tendons shifted and popped, and her bones lengthened and strengthened. Stability and swiftness, perfect balance and poise; her new frame simply *worked*.

And then, as easily as it had begun, the change was over, and Candance stood towering over Allen, clacking her teeth and chortling as best as she could with her new vocal cords.

Allen, to his great credit, hadn't moved an inch, though the whites of his eyes and the stench of fear sweat gave him away. "A raptor," he said, and swore. "Of course you had to be a raptor. We haven't seen a prehistoric mutation in decades, and now, just as we're getting the whole concept under control and starting to regulate it, you show up as a *bloody raptor.*"

Candance clacked her teeth again and attempted a laugh, which came out as more of a strangled roar than anything recognisably humorous—but Allen seemed to understand.

He rolled his eyes and shrugged himself away, huffing deeply. "Well, go on then. You'll have energy burning through your system like nothing else, if you're anything like normal. Go run it off somewhere people won't see you." He squeezed his eyes shut and massaged his temples. "And do me a favour, will you?"

Candance peered down at him, trying for any expression but hungry, because the finer details of emotions were beyond her at the moment. The power, the heat, the adrenalin surging through her veins and sizzling in her skin and making her want to run, and run, and run, and run...

Allen sighed resignedly. "Just come find me when you're yourself again? We need to talk." He glanced up at Candance, the first look he'd given her since he'd sworn at her—and immediately, he shook his head and walked away, hands deep down in his pockets.

The wind rolled in from the ocean, whipping up waves and bringing with it the promise of adventure.

Candance waited until Allen was nearly back inside, let her inner beast roar—just once, quietly—and sprinted away into the night.

THE MAKING OF *SHADOWS NEVER LIE*

I blame this one at least a little on Merc Fenn Wolfmoor, critically acclaimed short story writer and gem among human beings.

As a friend and critique partner in the late 2000s, Merc will always have my tremendous thanks for getting me through my first-ever novel, but this story in particular is Merc's responsibility because, around the time that a bunch of friends and I were attempting to practise the short-story form, Merc mentioned dinosaur shapeshifters.

I knew I had to try to do something with that. My first attempt, a noirish kind of piece, was fun to write, but I never managed to finish it.

Shadows Never Lie was my second attempt, and it was much more 'me' in its voice, and I had tremendous fun. One day, I might even revisit this world—it does seem rich in possibilities, doesn't it?

Read more by Amy Laurens!

TRUST ISSUES

WARM STEAM FILLED THE AIR AROUND Becca, faintly scented with fake apples from her shampoo. The hot water pattered down on her back, turning her skin red and, in theory, soothing away her tension. Of course, that would have been more easily facilitated had she not been in the midst of performing the contortions necessary to get her legs shaved, but she'd feel better once she was done. Probably.

Up, rinse, up, rinse; she scraped the blossom-pink razor over her pale legs, shaking it out in the main stream of the shower water at the top of each stroke. Steam billowed up in her face as she curled over her leg, warm against her cheeks and the inside of her nose.

There. Nearly done.

Honestly, the whole thing was an exercise in pointless futility. It wasn't like the wolf was going to be staring at her legs. And if he did, so what? Why did she care what he thought?

She didn't, that's what. Jaw clenching, Becca pressed shower water from her eye with the tips of her fingers.

One last stroke.

Becca inhaled sharply as the razor sliced the sensitive skin over her Achilles heel, removing a good slice of flesh and making the water run momentarily red.

She grabbed at her ankle with her free hand, trying to stem the bleeding with her thumb, and nearly slipped on the wet tiles. Her elbow smacked the bottles of hair products that lined the shower's shelf—and the shelf itself—and she hopped madly, trying to regain her balance. Her weight fell against the cold glass of the shower screen—and the door screaked open, dumping her unceremoniously on the mat.

"Ow." That was going to bruise her butt.

Disgusted, Becca threw the razor back into the shower and scrambled to her feet. She reached in and turned the water off, realising as she did that her right elbow was about as tender as her butt would be in the morning. She flung her dark blonde, wet hair out of her eyes. So much for getting pretty.

Stupid date.

Stupid wolf.

Red streaks on the mat caught her eye as she snagged her white towel off the rail: her heel, still dripping blood.

Bloody hell.

Literally.

She gathered her wet hair to one side, picking it off her shoulders and neck, wrapped the towel around herself, and hobbled to the vanity. Somewhere in there, lost amid cobwebbed piles of lotions, powders and unused potions, was a packet of bandaids.

Becca crouched awkwardly, stretching into the back of the cupboard that stank of bleach and toothpaste—and jumped as her sore elbow connected with something cold: a festering bottle of nail polish that was only too happy to jump off the shelf and smash on the floor, bleeding its awful browny-coral innards all over the second bath mat.

The chemical scent of the polish hit her nostrils. *Urgh. Someone remind me why I am doing this?*

Perching on the edge of the bath, Becca applied the bandaid, a giant strip wider than two of her fingers, its 'flesh' tones doing nothing to blend in with the complexion her grandmother had liked to call porcelain. "Bloody Irish," she muttered.

She smoothed the plaster down, snatched up the bloodied bathmat and took it to the laundry, then stalked back to her room to dress.

Underwear, now that was a question. Not that there was any *question* of him *seeing* her underwear. She was widowed, not desperate. Even if, just occasionally, when he turned his big stupid wolf eyes on her she lost her mind just a little bit remembering what sex had been like.

But back to the underwear, she reminded herself as she finished towelling off and used the damp towel to twist up her hair. She didn't trust him as far as she could throw him, which given she doubted she could even lift him off the ground amounted practically to not at all—but could she really bring herself to go plain black cotton on a date?

Ah, screw it. It wasn't like the dress was that fitted or anything. Comfy it was. Becca fished her favourite pair of black undies out from the crumpled mess in her top drawer, donned a sensible—if slightly uplifting—bra, and from the very back of her other top drawer snatched out an old, dusty satin pencil case, the magenta one with the floral embroidery.

Despite nearly stabbing herself in the eye with mascara she hadn't applied in years, and overdoing it with the big round hairbrush and the hairdryer so it looked like she was wearing a 1960s wig for a few minutes until she managed to de-volumise things a bit, Becca managed to finish getting ready with a relative minimum of fuss.

She slipped into her little black dress—always go with a classic on the first date, she'd decided; she still wasn't actually sure whether she wanted to impress the wolf or scare him away—slipped her phone, driver's licence and bank card into the cunningly placed pocket, straightened the short sleeves, and squished into a pair of heels that were dangerously tall and stunningly gorgeous: black satin with red and gold oriental designs brocaded into the fabric, nearly six inches high.

She wobbled for the first few steps before remembering how to balance right in them: Weight on the toes, pretend the shoes aren't really there, just tip-toe along with your calves tight and your core strong.

You got this.

She caught sight of her reflection in her dresser mirror and sighed, confidence deflating. It had been so long since she'd done this. She'd been married to that two-faced jerk Nick for nearly three years, but they'd dated for another four or five before that.

She hadn't first-dated since she was what, eighteen? Nineteen?

Becca ran a hand over her forehead and exhaled. Nick was gone now. He might have stolen eight years of her life and literally any chance she ever had at having children of her own—the familiar flutter of regret and longing trembled through her stomach—but he was gone.

And the wolf was safe, at least inasmuch as he wouldn't lie to her upfront like Nick had.

Probably.

Maybe.

She hoped.

Really, there was no way to know. And trust wasn't exactly her specialty, when she was used to being able to detect lies and secrets right there in the head of anybody around her.

Urgh. Why, why am I doing this? This is such a bad idea.

As if on cue, her phone buzzed.

A message from her sister Clare: *I know he's picking you up in fifteen minutes, which means you're moping around won-*

dering why you let me bully you into this, so I'm reminding you of our little bargain.

Besides. He's gorgeous. It'll be good for you.

Becca's lips quirked to a half smile. Her sister knew her all too well—hence the bargain, whereby Becca would be subjected to an endless stream of potential suitors every time she visited Clare if she didn't agree to a date with the wolf. And simply avoiding Clare's house wouldn't have worked; Clare would have just hauled the suitors to her.

A knock sounded at the door.

Adrenalin leapt through Becca's stomach and she bolted upright, stuffing her phone back into her pocket, then heading to the door.

"I'm sorry," Wolf-boy said as she opened it. "I know it's not fashionable to be early, but the traffic was better than I'd planned."

He'd left his longish hair down, a perfectly-styled tangle of honey-brown waves that screamed to be touched, and although he was wearing a dark suit, he'd left his baby-blue shirt open at the neck, and the combination did little to hide the sheer breadth and power of his shoulders.

His golden eyes drilled through her, soft and amused and completely, utterly focused on her.

Becca realised she was staring and closed her mouth, working the inside of her lower lip between her teeth.

So the wolf scrubbed up well. That changed nothing. She'd known since she'd met him that he was sex-on-legs. That, she'd learned the hard way, was not even *close* to the top ten most important things in a relationship. "It's okay," she said. "I'm ready."

She stepped out the door, forcing him to step aside for her, and locked up the house. "Ready?" The smile she gave him was too bright, brittle like it might crack any moment, and she tried to relax.

He studied her carefully for just an instant too long, but nodded. "Sure, let's go."

Keep reading! Head to
www.inkprintpress.com/amylaurens/
secretbreaker/trustissues/
to buy your copy now!

ABOUT THE AUTHOR

AMY LAURENS is an Australian author of fantasy fiction for all ages. She has never made a mess of herself at an awards ceremony, though shape-shifting is high on list of 'most-wanted superpowers' and would, she feels, be an acceptable excuse.

Amy has written the award-winning portal-fantasy *Sanctuary* series about Edge, a 13-year-old girl forced to move to a small country town because of witness protection (the first book is *Where Shadows Rise*), the humorous fantasy *Kaditeos* series, following newly graduated Evil Overlord Mercury as she attempts to acquire a castle, the young adult series *Storm Foxes*, about love and magic and family in small town Australia, and a whole host of non-fiction and shorter works.

INKLETS

Collect them all! Released on the 1st and 15th of each month.

Shadows
NEVER LIE
AMY LAURENS

Here She Lies
LIANA BROOKS

Perfect
Destruction
An Age Of Unicorns Story
AMY LAURENS

What Blood
Can Do
AMY LAURENS

Dancer, Dreamer
Seer
LIANA BROOKS

As Time
Whirls Slowly
Past
AMY LAURENS

Far More
Satisfying
Than Hell
AMY LAURENS

Just
Another Day
In Hell
LIANA BROOKS

Moon AND
Morning
AMY LAURENS

Some
Impropriety
Expected
AMY LAURENS

NEON SNOW
LIANA BROOKS

Reincarnation
LIANA BROOKS

More Than
Mushrooms
AMY LAURENS

DOUBLE ISSUE
How To Make A Star
& The World Ended
LIANA BROOKS

CAUGHT
IN THE ACT
AMY LAURENS

ANUBIS
Has Sent You
Six Souls
LIANA BROOKS

PRAYER TO A
GODDESS
LIANA BROOKS

Love In The
Time Of Corona
AMY LAURENS